TO
THOMAS
LOVE
TINA

CHRISTMA'S 1996

Moonlight on the River

Moonlight on the River

Words by Deborah Kovacs

Pictures by William Shattuck

Viking

The art was prepared on Stonehenge Rising paper,
using General's charcoal pencils and Grumbacher powdered charcoal.

VIKING
Published by the Penguin Group
Penguin Books USA Inc., 375 Hudson Street, New York, New York 10014, U.S.A.
Penguin Books Ltd, 27 Wrights Lane, London W8 5TZ, England
Penguin Books Australia Ltd, Ringwood, Victoria, Australia
Penguin Books Canada Ltd, 10 Alcorn Avenue, Toronto, Ontario, Canada M4V 3B2
Penguin Books (N.Z.) Ltd, 182–190 Wairau Road, Auckland 10, New Zealand

Penguin Books Ltd, Registered Offices: Harmondsworth, Middlesex, England

First published in 1993 by Viking, a division of Penguin Books USA Inc.

10 9 8 7 6 5 4 3 2 1

Text copyright © Deborah Kovacs, 1993
Illustrations copyright © William Shattuck, 1993
All rights reserved

Title calligraphy by Leah Palmer Preiss

Library of Congress Cataloging-in-Publication Data
Kovacs, Deborah. Moonlight on the river / by Deborah Kovacs;
illustrated by William Shattuck.   p.   cm.
Summary: Sneaking away from home on a midnight fishing
voyage, two brothers find themselves struggling to keep
their boat afloat in the middle of a violent river storm.
I S B N 0 - 6 7 0 - 8 4 4 6 3 - 2
[1. Rivers—Fiction. 2. Sailing—Fiction. 3. Fishing—Fiction.]
I. Shattuck, William, ill. II. Title.
PZ7.K8565Mo 1993 [E]—dc20   92-28377 CIP AC

Printed in U.S.A.   Set in 16 point Goudy Old Style
Without limiting the rights under copyright reserved above, no part of this
publication may be reproduced, stored in or introduced into a retrieval system,
or transmitted, in any form or by any means (electronic, mechanical,
photocopying, recording or otherwise), without the prior written permission
of both the copyright owner and the above publisher of this book.

For my family,
and also for the River
in its timeless beauty.
As it was, as it is, may it ever be.

—D.K.

To my sons Will and Ben and their Ma.
May moonlight always shine on you
and may the river always bring you home.

—W.S.

The moon was full and midnight high.
Ben shook Will.
"It's time to go," he said.

Will finished packing
and threw the heavy bag over his shoulder.
Moving silently so they wouldn't wake their parents
the brothers slipped outside.

The night was filled
with deep green smells
and animal sounds.
The air was as warm as a bath.
The ground felt damp and slippery on their bare feet
as Ben and Will ran down the mossy slope to the river.

There, the sailboat waited.
It tugged at its moorings,
riding the rising tide.

With a swish, a restless fish
broke the river's calm surface.
"Hear that?" said Will,
as they boarded the boat.

Will tied a hook and
a fishing line to the stern,
then watched as the hook
dropped into the depths.
"You'll see, Ben," he said.
"The blues always bite
when the moon is full."

Soon they were sailing
up the smooth, wide river.
A great blue heron
shrieked farewell.

Will manned the tiller.
Ben held the sheets.
The sail billowed under the light breeze.
The little boat moved swiftly
up the river's deepest channel.

Ben watched nighttime shapes rise all about him.
Everything looked different in the darkness—
bigger, blacker, full of shadows.
Ben blinked as his eyes played tricks.
He edged closer to Will.

In the night's velvet light, Will could scarcely see
the break in the spartina grass.
The rushes seemed to loom larger,
the branches to dip lower.
Will grasped the tiller tightly,
his palms damp with sweat.
Was this the way in?

At last they broke through into the still cove.

Will peered over the side of the boat.

He moved the stern line up and down.

Ben dipped his hand in the cool water,

stirring up tiny creatures

that glowed with phosphorescence.

"The fish are here, just like you said," whispered Ben.

In the cove, the bluefish swam in a tight circle,
their fins and tails lit by moon glow and fireflies.
Will kept moving the line.
For a long, still hour, nothing bit.

Will looked up at the moon,
now a tiny circle high in the sky.
"We can't stay here," he said.
"The tide's turning,
and we've got to go downriver."

Ben's head felt heavy.
He sank beneath a blanket of coat,
and made his arms his pillow.
"I'll stay awake," said Will.

Will guided the boat through the narrows
and tacked south, heading for home.
Alert, alone, he inhaled deeply.
Had the night air changed?
Did he smell rain?

Suddenly, Will's breath was broken
by a rise in the wind
that raised the waves
and wet the deck.
Keep her steady, he thought.

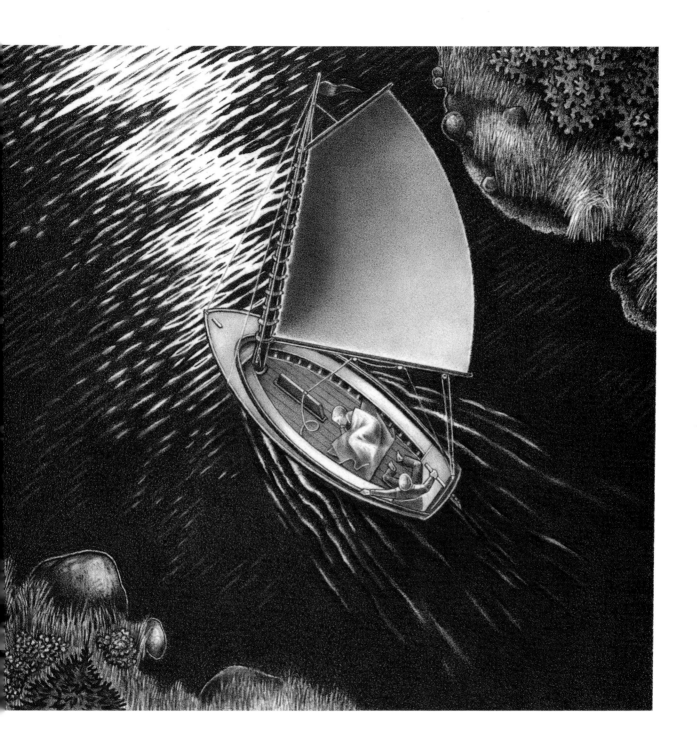

When they reached the open water, the wind was huge.
The sail began to flap, moving crazily back and forth.
"Ben!" called Will.

Ben woke up, ready to help.
He hauled the sheet.
Will manned the tiller.
Still the water grew rougher.

A chill rain fell, its sharp drops shattering on the deck.

The boat heeled in the rising wind.

Overboard went coat and book, socks and food.

Breathing quickly, Ben watched Will.

Will knew he must stay calm.

"We've got to get off the river!" he shouted.

Now the storm surrounded them.
Through the darkness and churning water,
through the mist and salty spray,
Will saw another boat.
It was much like theirs, except
there was only one man on deck.
He stood tall and steady,
his arm pointing to starboard.
Was he guiding them to an inlet?
"Let's head to starboard," called Will.

In minutes, a safe cove sheltered them.
Ben dropped the anchor.
Will tied the stern line to a tree.
They huddled beneath a tarp,
waiting for the storm to pass.

"Keep a lookout for that other boat," Will told Ben.
But all they could see was rain and lightning,
and all they could hear was thunder
and the roar of the wind.

Just before dawn, the waves rested at last.

As Ben hauled the anchor,

Will went ashore to untie the stern line.

We've got to remember this spot, he thought.

He wished he had a penknife to mark the big old beech tree.

But there was no need, for someone had been there before them.

The boys sailed home in a steady breeze.
Ben scanned the horizon, and saw that they sailed alone.

As Ben tied the boat to the mooring,
the forgotten fishing line
snapped with a strike.
Will laughed as he hauled in
a five-pound blue.
The brothers crept up the lawn,
Will carrying his prize.
They crawled through
their open bedroom window
as the sky began to lighten.

Shivering, they changed to warm pajamas
and curled into their beds.

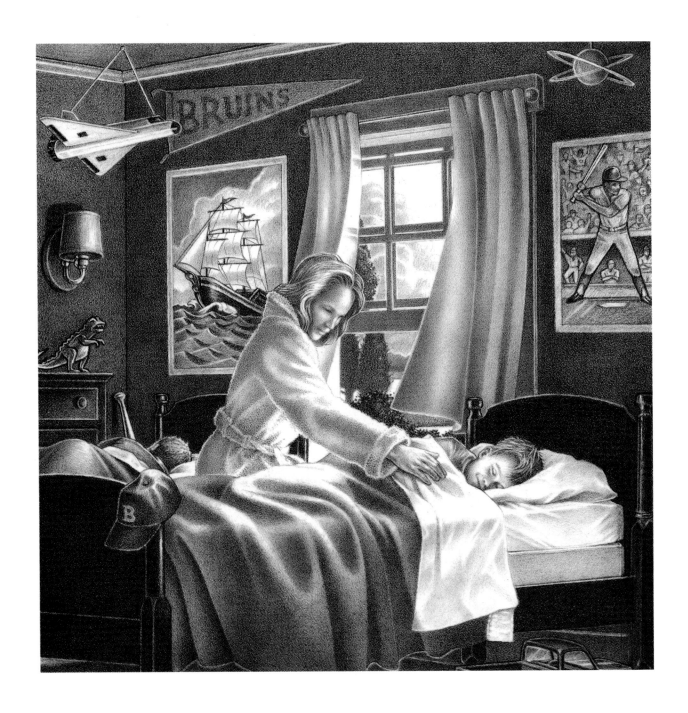

When their mother came to wake them,
she saw the fish on the bedroom floor.
What were those boys up to? she wondered.

Then she knew. For she was once a girl
on the smooth, wide river.
She smiled as she looked out at the calm water
that had delivered her children home safely.

The river was quiet now.
It stretched beneath the daylight,
sparkling with the memory of journeys past
and the possibility of adventures yet to come.